Withdrawn

Dear Parent:

Congratulations! Your child is taking
the first steps on an exciting journey.
The destination? Independent reading!

STEP INTO READING® will help your child get there. The program offers
books at five levels that accompany children from their first attempts at
reading to reading success. Each step includes fun stories, fiction and
nonfiction, and colorful art. There are also Step into Reading Sticker Books,
Step into Reading Math Readers, and Step into Reading Phonics Readers—
a complete literacy program with something to interest every child.

Learning to Read, Step by Step!

Ready to Read   Preschool–Kindergarten
• big type and easy words • rhyme and rhythm • picture clues
For children who know the alphabet and are eager to
begin reading.

Reading with Help   Preschool–Grade 1
• basic vocabulary • short sentences • simple stories
For children who recognize familiar words and sound out
new words with help.

Reading on Your Own   Grades 1–3
• engaging characters • easy-to-follow plots • popular topics
For children who are ready to read on their own.

Reading Paragraphs   Grades 2–3
• challenging vocabulary • short paragraphs • exciting stories
For newly independent readers who read simple sentences
with confidence.

Ready for Chapters   Grades 2–4
• chapters • longer paragraphs • full-color art
For children who want to take the plunge into chapter books
but still like colorful pictures.

STEP INTO READING® is designed to give every child a successful
reading experience. The grade levels are only guides. Children can progress
through the steps at their own speed, developing confidence in their
reading, no matter what their grade.

Remember, a lifetime love of reading starts with a single step!

For my Nanny, with love
—M.L.

www.stepintoreading.com

Educators and librarians, for a variety of teaching tools, visit us at www.randomhouse.com/teachers

Library of Congress Cataloging-in-Publication Data
Lagonegro, Melissa.
As you wish / by Melissa Lagonegro.
    p. cm. — (Step into reading. A step 1 book)
Summary: Aladdin, Jasmine, and Abu the monkey make all sorts of wishes, from a bouquet of flowers to a trip to the moon, and the Genie makes them come true.
ISBN 0-7364-2244-7 — ISBN 0-7364-8032-3 (Gibraltar lib. ed.)
[1. Magic — Fiction. 2. Wishes — Fiction. 3. Stories in rhyme.] I. Title. II. Series: Step into reading. Step 1 book.
PZ8.3.L1363As 2004 [E] — dc22 2003013087

Printed in the United States of America   10 9 8 7 6 5 4 3 2 1

STEP INTO READING, RANDOM HOUSE, and the Random House colophon are registered trademarks and the Step into Reading colophon is a trademark of Random House, Inc.

Disney's Aladdin

As You Wish

by Melissa Lagonegro

illustrated by Atelier Philippe Harchy

Random House 🏠 New York

Far away,
across the sea,
lives a kind
and great Genie.

Rub the lamp.

See him rise.

Poof, poof, poof,
out he flies.

What you wish
is what you get.

Just three wishes.

Don't forget!

With a poof

and a puff

and a big kaboom . . .

. . . the Genie can
make flowers bloom!

He can fill a room
with lots of gold.

He can make it hot . . .

. . . or very cold.

Jasmine wishes
to go to the moon.

And take a ride
in a big balloon.

21

She wants a dress
of pink and blue.

Poof!

The Genie makes her

dreams come true.

Aladdin wants
to sail the seas.

And swing up high
among the trees.

Just one more wish.
What will it be?

A thank-you gift
for the Genie!

What will your three wishes be?